WELCOME HOME, BARNEY

Barney the bat lived all on his own.
No mum and dad.
No sisters and brothers.
No mate, to mate with.
Barney was the loneliest bat
in the world.

Barney was lonely
because he was the *only*
large mouse–eared bat left
in the country.
Barney didn't know that.

He thought there must be
other bats, just like him,
somewhere, out there.
He kept hoping he would find one.

Each night, when Barney went out,
searching for food,
he kept one eye open
searching for a mate.

WELCOME
HOME, BARNEY

The Loneliest Bat
in the World.

Rose Impey
Shoo Rayner

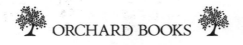

ORCHARD BOOKS

ORCHARD BOOKS
96 Leonard Street, London EC2A 4RH
Orchard Books Australia
14 Mars Road, Lane Cove, NSW 2066
First published in Great Britain 1995
First paperback publication 1995
Text © Rose Impey 1995
Illustrations © Shoo Rayner 1995
The right of Rose Impey to be identified as the Author
and Shoo Rayner as the Illustrator of this Work has
been asserted by them in accordance with the
Copyright, Designs and Patents Act, 1988.
A CIP catalogue record for this book
is available from the British Library.
1 85213 765 7 (hardback)
1 85213 769 X (paperback)
Printed in Great Britain by
The Guernsey Press Co. Ltd, Guernsey, C.I.

But each night he came home
without one.

Barney had friends, of course,
Owl and Rat and Spider.
"Cheer up," they said.
"You've always got us."
But no matter how hard they tried
they couldn't cheer him up.

"Why don't you take a holiday?"
said Owl.

Travel around.
Visit other places.

So Barney took Owl's advice.

Barney travelled all over Britain.
But it didn't suit him.

He got travelsick.
He got homesick.
He got lonely.
Barney came home,
all alone.

"You should pull yourself together,"
said Spider.

Barney didn't have *an image*.
He thought he'd better get one.

Barney tried to be cool.

He tried to be punk.

He tried to be sporty.

But nothing seemed to suit him.
He felt silly
and embarrassed
and lonely.
Barney came home,
all alone.

"You're too fussy," said Rat.
"There are lots of other bats
to choose from."

I'll find you a girl.

Barney blushed.
He was very shy.
Even when he found a girl,
he wouldn't know what to say to her.

Rat talked to his friends.

He advertised in the newspaper.

Heartbroken Hedgehog—
prickly outside but soft underneath.
looking for friendship and cuddles.

Mature Mouse—
wants to meet intelligent opera lover.
Two tickets for Die Fleidermouse.

LONELY
Large Mouse-Eared Bat
Seeks
Lady Bat
for
lifetime partnership.
Serious replies
only
P. O. Box 123

Dashing Dog—
own teeth and hair—
looking for beautiful bitch.
Ring Barking 367

Lonely Owl—
Too sad to give a hoot—
wants flying partner. 28-28-200

He even wrote to Batline.

Rat found lots of girls.
But none of them suited Barney.

Pippi was a pipistrelle bat.
She was too small.

Freda was a fruit bat.
She was a vegetarian.

Err!

Vera was a vampire bat.
She sucked blood!
That didn't suit Barney.

"I'm sorry," he told Rat.
"It's not that I'm fussy.
They're all very nice bats,
but they're not like me."

"Well, never mind," said Rat.
"You've always got your friends."
But it still didn't cheer him up.
Barney hung in the dark
feeling sorry for himself,
all on his own.

It was okay for Owl,
he had a mate.
She had a nest full of baby owls.
Owl had a family.

It was okay for Spider.
She'd made an egg sac
with hundreds of baby spiders
in it.
Soon Spider would have
an *enormous* family.

And it was okay for Rat.
Rat had dozens and dozens
of relations.
Rat's family filled the barn.
They were always having
family celebrations.

But Barney had no one
— no one special.
No one to hunt with.
No one to hang out with.
No one to say goodnight to.
Barney was the loneliest
bat in the world.

Then one day Barney woke up.
He was fed up with feeling
sorry for himself.
He decided to do something about it.

Barney hired a private detective,
a mole called Mortimer.

Mortimer sniffed out all the clues
he could find.

"Which do you want first,"
said Mortimer, "the good news
or the bad news?"
"The bad news," said Barney, sadly.
"Well, you're the only one,
I'm afraid. The last of the line."
"The last?" said Barney.

Mortimer nodded.
"You're the last large mouse–eared
bat in the country."
Barney was so disappointed
he started to cry.

"Now, don't get upset," said Mortimer.

The good news is:
There are other bats like you,
lots of them,
all over Europe.
You'll have to go abroad,
if you want to find them.

Barney was nervous.
He had never been abroad before.
He might get travelsick.
He might get homesick.
He might get lost.

31

"And we'll all be here,
when you get back," they told him.
That cheered Barney up.

So Barney bought his ticket
and sent for his passport.
He said goodbye to his friends
and flew to France.

33

When he got there he found
lots of bats like him.
They were very pleased to meet him.

Barney travelled around Germany

and Spain

and Greece.

Wherever he went there were
different places to hunt,
different food to eat,
different bats to meet.

Lots of girl bats too.
Bella and Bobbie and Bernie.

They each wanted Barney
to stay with them
and settle down,
but he couldn't.

Barney was feeling homesick again.
He had travelled a long way
and found just what he was
looking for.
But all he wanted was to go home.

Barney missed his barn.
He missed the peace and quiet
of his own life.
He missed his friends.

He wondered what they were doing,
back in the barn, without him.

Barney realised for the first time
how much he liked
his life at home.
In the end, Barney knew
he would have to choose.

Barney the bat packed his bags,
said goodbye to his new friends
and caught the next plane home.

Barney was pleased to be home.
And his friends were pleased
to see him.
They gave him a Welcome Home party.
"Tell us all about it," said Owl.
"Did you find a girl?" said Rat.
"You look *different*," said Spider.

Barney showed them his photos.
He gave them their presents.
He told them how much
he'd missed them.

"It was a good trip,"
Barney told his new friend, Mortimer.
"But I'm glad to be back.
East or West, home is best.
And home is where your friends are."
"Here's to friendship," said Mortimer.

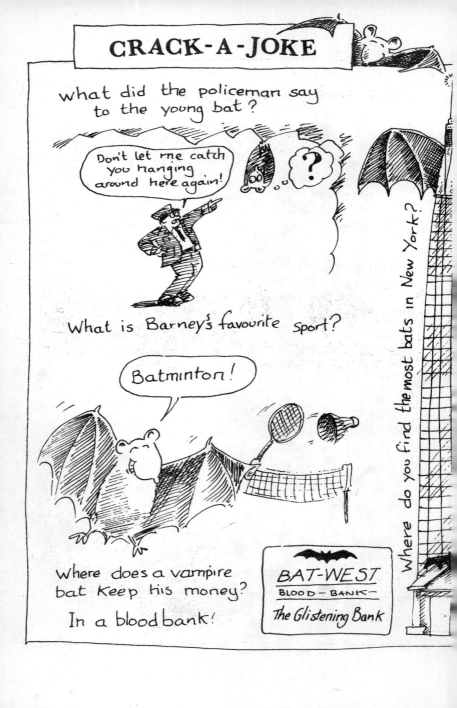

What fruit do vampire bats like best?

Blood oranges   and   Neck-tarines.

Where do vampire bats go after the movies?

SHOWING TONIGHT
BATMAN

Out for a bite!

In the Vampire State Building

What can a toothless vampire do?

Give you a nasty suck!

What does a polite vampire say?

Fang you very much!

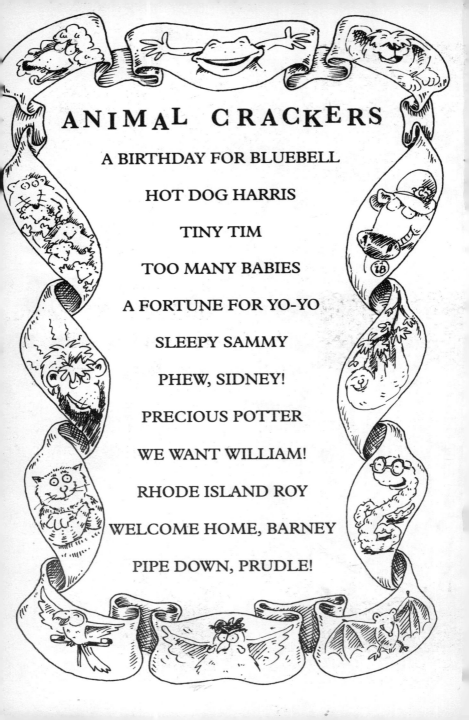

ANIMAL CRACKERS

A BIRTHDAY FOR BLUEBELL

HOT DOG HARRIS

TINY TIM

TOO MANY BABIES

A FORTUNE FOR YO-YO

SLEEPY SAMMY

PHEW, SIDNEY!

PRECIOUS POTTER

WE WANT WILLIAM!

RHODE ISLAND ROY

WELCOME HOME, BARNEY

PIPE DOWN, PRUDLE!